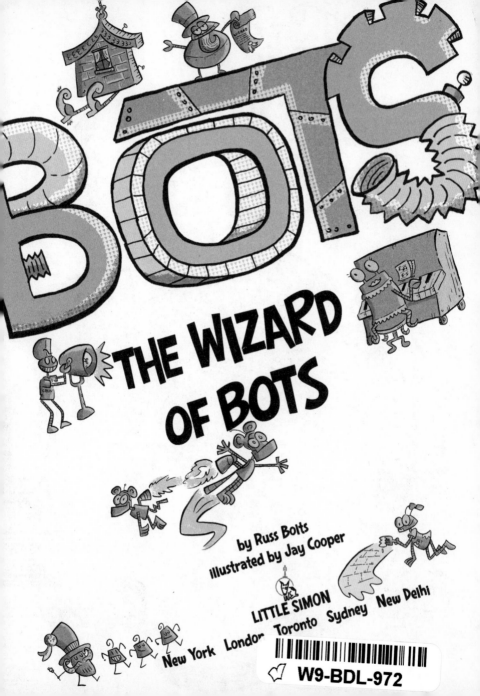

BOTS

THE WIZARD OF BOTS

by Russ Bolts
Illustrated by Jay Cooper

LITTLE SIMON

New York London Toronto Sydney New Delhi

This book is a work of fiction. Any references to historical events, real people, or real places are used fictitiously. Other names, characters, places, and events are products of the author's imagination, and any resemblance to actual events or places or persons, living or dead, is entirely coincidental.

LITTLE SIMON

An imprint of Simon & Schuster Children's Publishing Division • 1230 Avenue of the Americas, New York, New York 10020 • First Little Simon paperback edition April 2021 • Copyright © 2021 by Simon & Schuster, Inc. Also available in a Little Simon hardcover edition. All rights reserved, including the right of reproduction in whole or in part in any form. LITTLE SIMON is a registered trademark of Simon & Schuster, Inc., and associated colophon is a trademark of Simon & Schuster, Inc. For information about special discounts for bulk purchases, please contact Simon & Schuster Special Sales at 1-866-506-1949 or business@simonandschuster.com. The Simon & Schuster Speakers Bureau can bring authors to your live event. For more information or to book an event contact the Simon & Schuster Speakers Bureau at 1-866-248-3049 or visit our website at www.simonspeakers.com. Manufactured in the United States of America 0221 MTN

2   4   6   8   10   9   7   5   3   1

Cataloging-in-Publication Data is available for this title from the Library of Congress.

ISBN 978-1-5344-8639-3 (pbk)
ISBN 978-1-5344-8640-9 (hc)
ISBN 978-1-5344-8641-6 (eBook)

CONTENTS

CHAPTER 1

Acting!

DARKNESS.
IN THIS MOMENT,
ANYTHING IS
POSSIBLE.

THE STAGE IS SET.

THE WORLD IS WAITING TO SEE WHAT WILL HAPPEN NEXT.

AND THEN...

THERE, NOW THAT I HAVE YOUR ATTENTION, I WANT TO TALK ABOUT...

ACTING!

WHO KNOWS WHAT ACTING IS?

YES?

UM, ACTING IS LIKE PRETENDING.

20

34

CHAPTER 4 Astro-Munchkins

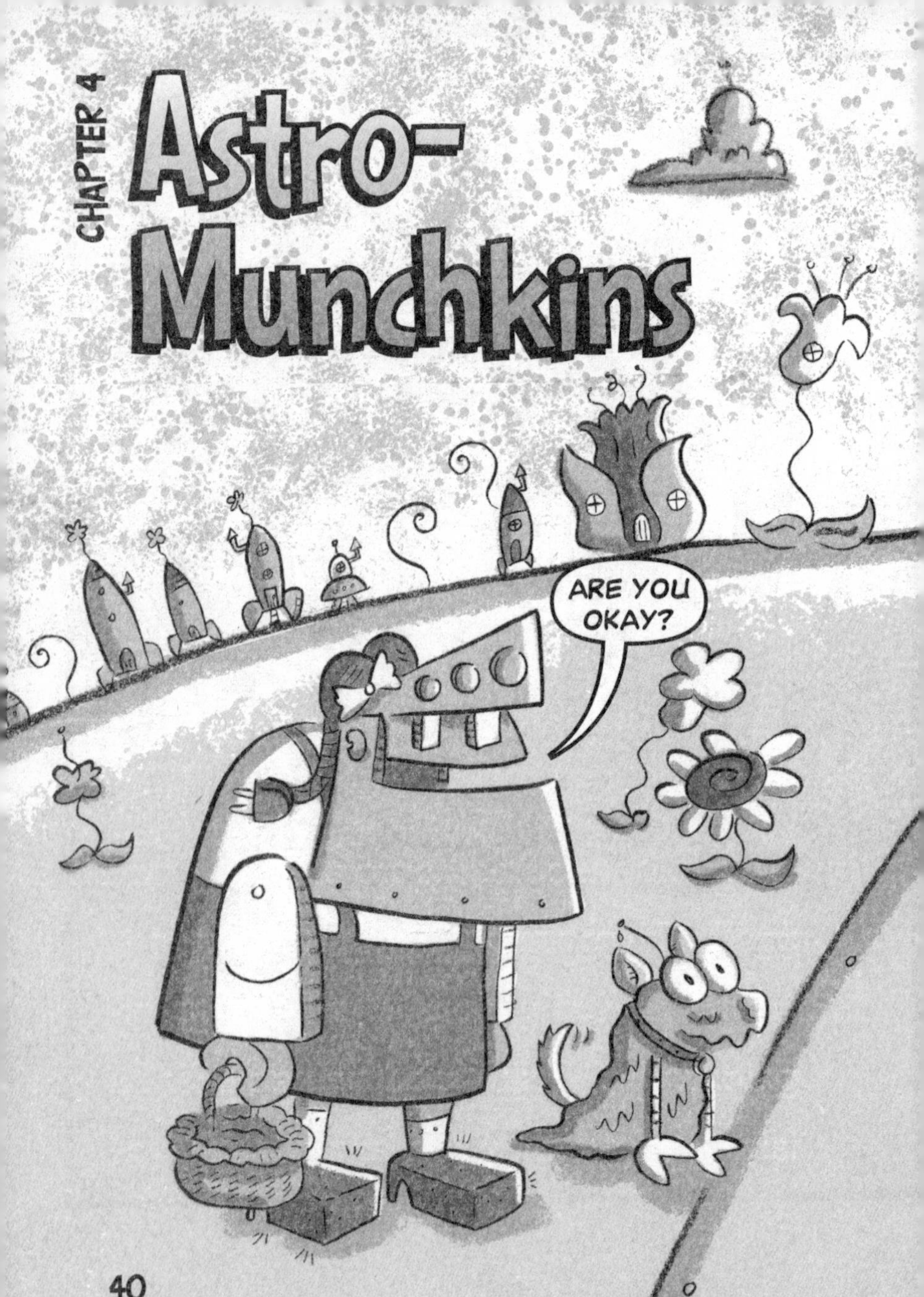

41

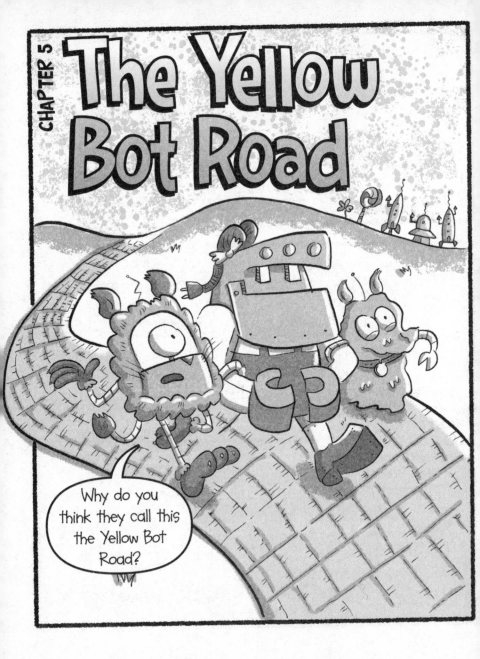

55

Wicked Tinny

63

65

66

68

69

75

77

GRAB!

SNATCH!

WOOF. NOPE, THEY ARE NOT NICER. WOOF.

TAKE!

CHAPTER 8

The Wizard

If you're looking for the wizard, he lives right next door. People mix up our castles all the time.

BIG BATTLE DAY

-Put water in large pot
 -Boil
  -Toil
  -Trouble

      -Feed cat
       -Clean litter box
-Gather spells at the spell store
     -Buy more warts
     -Need newt eyes

-Dust the castle with more dust
-Add spiderwebs to every corner
     -Get Dorothy
     -And her little dog, too
          -A present

Here we are.

CHAPTER 9

The Show Must Go On

Come on, guys. You're not really going to listen to him, are you?

I mean, I'm magic too. I can help you.

Plus we're like best friends, right? Remember when I attacked you with Flying Monkey Bots? Wasn't that cool?

114